✶✶✶✶ THE COBTOWN OBSERVER

TOWN NOTICES:
Fliberty Jibbert says that whoever left off a brown boot with a broken heel, can come and get it. It is as good as new now. ✶ ✶

The Cobtown Militia will not ha practice do Beaver M week beca monster be

---

There will service un due to ro tracks near

THAT'S
THEY
We have
Children o
what they
Adapulgus
This is what they say:
✶ I bet it's got the head of an alligator and the body of a lion and the claws of an eagle!
— Jasper Payne
✶ I think it is big and scaly like a lizard, spits fire and stinks real bad!
— Shadrack Dingle

✶ I don't know what it looks like, but my Pa says 25 cents is a awful lot of money to find out.
— Valentine McGinty
✶ I know it is big, strong and fierce. That is enough. It

EX LIBRIS

SOUTH ORANGE
PUBLIC LIBRARY

ELIXIR ✶
It's all natural *and tastes good too!*
IF YOU WANT IT, WE HAVE GOT IT!
— at the —
GENERAL STORE.
J. Ravenell, Prop.

Payne's Inn & Tavern. Fine Food ,Drink, Beds. and no Monsters! In the heart of Cobtown.

HEDDY PEGGLER

OINKEY

LUCKY HART

JASPER PAYNE

FLIBERTY JIBBERT

THE MONSTER IN THE SHADOWS

A COBTOWN® STORY
From the Diaries of Lucky Hart

Written by
JULIA VAN NUTT

Illustrated by
ROBERT VAN NUTT

A Doubleday Book for Young Readers

VALENTINE McGINTY

PROFESSOR McGINTY

SHORT TOOTH   SAMSON   CAPT. RAGG   MUDDY & BUDDY

For Robert, who is half Fliberty and
half Oinkey and altogether wonderful
J.V.N.

For Julia, who made me lucky when,
long ago, she captured my heart
R.V.N.

A DOUBLEDAY BOOK FOR YOUNG READERS
Published by Random House Children's Books
a division of Random House, Inc.
1540 Broadway
New York, New York 10036
Doubleday and the anchor with dolphin colophon are trademarks of
Random House, Inc.
Text copyright © 2000 by Julia Van Nutt
Illustrations copyright © 2000 by Robert Van Nutt

Cataloging-in-Publication Data is available from the Library of Congress.
ISBN: 0-385-32565-7

The text of this book is set in 15-point Greg.
Book design by Robert Van Nutt

Manufactured in the United States of America
September 2000
10 9 8 7 6 5 4 3 2 1

Vital Sparks

"Take this box of old medicine out to the garbage," Grandma told me. Her voice was muffled because her head and shoulders were inside the bathroom closet. Various bottles came zooming out and landed in the box.

I picked up a bottle bearing a label that read "Wampum Oil, the Indians' Elixir of Life." Another one read "Princess Moonbeam's Vital Sparks, God's Gift to Men."

"They don't carry this brand in the stores anymore, do they?" I asked.

"They never did," Grandma said. "That was sold to your grandpa by Princess Moonbeam herself. She used to pass this way every couple of years with her traveling show."

"Let me get this straight," I said. "You and Grandpa bought cures from traveling medicine shows?"

"Grandpa, me and just about everybody else around here," said Grandma. "Those folks sold dreams. You didn't always end up cured, but they always ended up with your money. They were mighty entertaining, too. If you want a good story about these traveling shows, go up in the attic. My grandmother Lucky Hart wrote about it in one of her diaries. Dig into the old green trunk and look for the book with the tattered cover. You'll learn a few tricks from that one, you will. Now, run along, I've got to keep to my work."

Thursday morning

    Lots of remarkable animals have visited Cobtown. Some came and never wanted to leave. Oinkey the wild pig feels that way, I'm sure.

    Today we learned that yet another wild beast is in town. It is called an Adapulgus. Nobody from Cobtown ever heard of one or knows what it looks like. We think it's big. We think it's strong. We know we are scared and with good reason. This is how it all started.

    I went over to Fliberty Jibbert's this morning. He has worked for my family most of his life and can fix just about anything. His sign reads "Shoe Repair for Man or Beast" but he can do much more than that.

Fliberty Jibbert

MYSTERY MONSTER COMES TO COBTOWN!
This Friday evening.

My good friend Jasper Payne was there too. He was sitting near the fire putting on his boots that had just been mended. Fliberty, who was starting work on a horseshoe, was making the fire glow hotter by blowing on it with his bellows. Whish, whish, whish, the bellows breathed like a panting beast.

I sat down by Jasper. "Have you ever seen Fliberty make his hand-shadow pictures on the wall?" I asked.

"Of course I have. Ever see him make a goat shadow?"

"Sure, plenty of times. Did you ever see Fliberty make a bird shadow that seems to fly?" I asked.

Fliberty laughed. "Sounds like I need some fresh material for your entertainment. Bet you've never seen this." He took his two hands and made a rabbit appear on the wall. The rabbit rubbed its ears with its paws.

"Now, what's this?" Fliberty asked as he made a little shadow-pig run.

We heard something go "Oink, oink." It was not a shadow-beast but a real living pig.

"Well, look who's here, Lucky—your aunt Heddy and Oinkey," Fliberty announced as those two walked in.

"Good morning," Heddy greeted us. "I've come to see if you can mend this hole in my kettle."

Fliberty nodded. "I expect so. I was just about to show Lucky and Jasper one of my best donkey tricks. Want to watch?"

"Your best donkey trick? Who could refuse such an offer?" said Aunt Heddy.

Fliberty smiled and turned his bellows away from the fire and towards Muddy and Buddy, two of his donkeys. He pumped up and down on the bellows with his foot. Whish, whish, whish, went the bellows, puffing air right into the donkeys' faces. It tickled them so much that they started kicking out behind them. Bam! bam! bam! went their hoofs against the wooden wall.

Then Muddy and Buddy let loose with a bray that made our ears ring. "EEE-Haw! EEE-Haw!" they said.

All the commotion got Oinkey excited and he started squealing, "EEEEEEE! EEEEEE!" Altogether, they made quite a racket. It seemed as if they wanted more. We laughed so hard that Fliberty sent another puff of air into their faces. It was all so much fun.

Bam! bam!   EEE-Haw!   EEE-Haw!   EEEEEE!   EEEEE!

Muddy   Buddy   Oinkey

A short while later a stranger came into Fliberty's. He was a big man—at least some of him was big (his hands, his stomach and his voice).

"Allow me to introduce myself. I am Captain Ragg," said the man. "Your sign says you do repair work for beasts. Can you fix this?" He handed Fliberty a huge harness. It was torn in two.

Fliberty took one look at the harness and said, "I can fix it, but tell me, what kind of critter broke through this thick leather?"

"The savage beast that destroyed this harness is in my tent down at the Beaver Meadow. It is an Adapulgus. The dangerous creature is asleep for the moment. I urge you to make the repair quickly. I must get this harness back on the blood-thirsty monster before it awakens and tries to escape," he said.

We agreed that fixing the harness for this Adapulgus seemed more urgent than mending a kettle. So Aunt Heddy, Jasper, Oinkey and I all left together.

"Aunt Heddy," I asked, "what's an Adapulgus?"

She shook her head and said, "In all my years, I've never heard of one. But whatever it is, it's here in Cobtown now!"

Thursday night

   This evening, there was a commotion right in the middle of town. It was that Captain Ragg. He had another fellow with him who was giving out handbills.

   The Captain had an old dog by his side, too. That pitiful creature was tied to the end of a rope. He was boney, his knees quivered and he held his tail down between his legs and wouldn't look up.

   Captain Ragg blew a tin horn as hard as he could. The other fellow lit two torches and we gathered around the Captain as he spoke.

   "Good evening, folks. I have amazing news! Me and Short Tooth have captured one of the fiercest beasts to ever walk the earth!"

   "Is Short Tooth that old dog?" Jasper asked him.

   "No, boy, Short Tooth is my assistant." He nodded towards the fellow holding the torches. "This noble beast is Samson, and not long ago he was the bravest dog in the world. But look at him now."

"What happened?" I asked.

"You may well ask, little girl," Captain Ragg said as he turned to me. "This once noble animal was reduced to the sorry critter you see before you by the Adapulgus! I'm talking about the one and only Adapulgus. Why, he's so mean he eats live polecats in one gulp. And he can swallow a tumblin' tumbleweed, briars and all, without needin' a drink of water to wash it down.

"It happened far off, in the Indian Territory, where Samson cornered that savage monster. Why, it took thirty-five hunters with ropes to pull them apart. By thunder! It was one terrible fight, but we finally got the Adapulgus tied down.

"Now, me and Short Tooth are here to tell you that you can see the mighty Adapulgus in our tent down in the Beaver Meadow tomorrow night."

BEHOLD!
THE BEAST
Known only
in Legend!
Never Before
✳ **Held in** ✳
CAPTIVITY!
══ THE ══
ADAPULGUS
✳ **ALIVE!** ✳
One Night Only!
✳ **FRIDAY** ✳
At the Beaver Meadow
25 cents

This news made us all nervous. My friend Valentine spoke up and said, "That sounds scary!"

"Scary? Sure it's scary, but are you too scared to take advantage of a once-in-a-lifetime opportunity?" said Captain Ragg. "Let me put your mind at ease." His eyes wandered across the crowd. "You, Fliberty Jibbert, step up here. I ask you, sir, did we do business together today?"

"Yes, we did," Fliberty said. "You brought in a harness for me to repair. It was the biggest one I ever saw, and it was torn apart."

"And repair it he did," Captain Ragg hollered. "You know this man and the good work that he does. Now this harness is stronger than ever. The Adapulgus will be wearing it tomorrow night when you come to gaze with jaw-droppin' wonder. Don't worry, folks, he can't break free! The show starts at six!"

Short Tooth plunged the torches into a rain barrel. Then he, Samson and Captain Ragg just seemed to vanish into the darkness.

It was spooky going home, and now I can see the Captain's tent from my window. They say the Adapulgus is in there. They say it is wearing the harness. Still, I am frightened. What if it breaks loose? What if I look out and see it?? What if it looks in and sees me???

Friday

All through the day I heard folks talking about the Adapulgus. Some want to see it and some, like Mama, do not. She says she doesn't want to see such a monster. She says she would feel better if Papa was not away traveling. Then he could take me. She will let me go as long as I'm with Aunt Heddy and Fliberty.

As darkness fell, we headed over to the Adapulgus tent. Jasper and the entire Payne family were there. Valentine McGinty and his family were just arriving. Everywhere I looked I saw people I knew. Everybody looked excited.

Captain Ragg stood outside the tent. He collected our money and gave us handbills as we entered. He looked happy and not at all frightened.

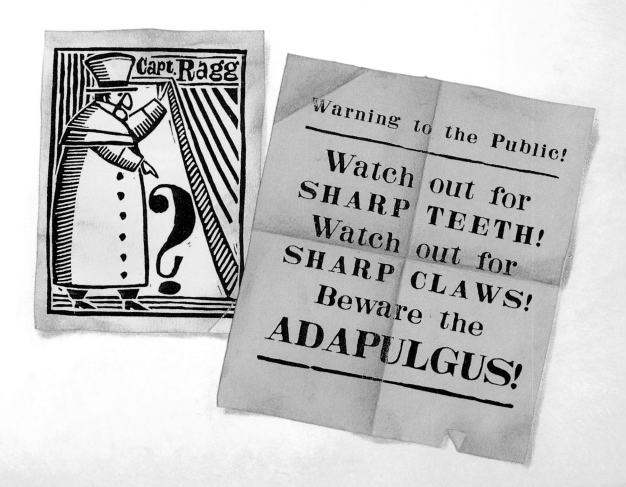

We took our seats and tried to read our handbills. It was hard to concentrate because we could hear the Adapulgus growling behind a curtain. The sounds were deep and frightening. The walls of the tent seemed to swell out from the beast's monstrous cries.

"Does the Adapulgus have sharp claws?" I asked Fliberty. "Can he run fast?"

Before he could answer, Jasper leaned over and said, "I bet his mouth is so big, he can bite your head off with one chomp!"

"He can run faster than a horse! He can eat a whole horse in one bite," Valentine told us.

"How do you know?" I asked them.

But before I could get a straight answer, Captain Ragg marched up to the curtain. A big gust of wind shook the tent, and the growling got louder. I grabbed Aunt Heddy's hand and was about to tell her I had decided NOT to see the Adapulgus when Captain Ragg addressed the crowd. "Ladies and gentlemen, tonight you are about to witness—"

All of a sudden we heard Short Tooth cry out from behind the curtain, "Captain! Come quick!"

A worried look passed over Captain Ragg's face.

"One moment, please!" he shouted before diving out of sight.

Warning to the Public!
Watch out for
SHARP TEETH!
Watch out for
SHARP CLAWS!
Beware the
ADAPULGUS!

Warning to the Public!
Watch out for
SHARP TEETH!
Watch out for
SHARP CLAWS!
Beware the
ADAPULGUS!

Just as he disappeared, a terrific bellowing started up.
A dog barked and howled. Chains clanked. The wind made
the lanterns sway back and forth. I grabbed Fliberty's
hand.

Then the curtain started shaking and we heard the
Captain's voice yell, "Oh! Hold fast, Short Tooth! Hit
him on the head! Go on! He'll break free! Ahhhhh, THERE
HE GOES!"

Captain Ragg and Short Tooth rushed out from
behind the curtain and shouted, "RUN FOR YOUR
LIVES, THE ADAPULGUS IS LOOSE! Return to your
homes and lock the doors. Stay inside if you value your
lives!"

We all ran out, shrieking and yelling.

"Come with me!" Fliberty grabbed both me and Aunt
Heddy. "My place is closest. I've got to see if the
animals are safe. Oinkey was there when I left."

We ran as fast as we could. A low fire was still burning
in Fliberty's hearth, and the donkeys were calm. Oinkey
was peacefully sleeping. Suddenly we heard a shuffling
sound. "It's the Adapulgus!" I whispered.

Fliberty put his fingers up to his lips and the three of us stepped back into the dark shadows. Oinkey woke up and pushed next to Aunt Heddy. My heart was pounding so hard that I feared the Adapulgus would hear it.

"Short Tooth, this way." It was Captain Ragg. We saw him, Short Tooth and Samson approach. The Adapulgus was nowhere in sight.

Aunt Heddy was about to speak up when we heard Short Tooth laugh. "I reckon them fools is all in their homes, locked up tight and too afraid to even peep out of their windows. Heh, heh," he sniggered. "That sure is a good trick, Captain. They all believed it. Why, I almost believed it myself."

The Captain pulled a sack of coins out of his vest and shook it. "Stick with me and we can fleece every fool town we visit," he said. He opened the sack and started counting the money.

Fliberty looked over at Aunt Heddy. I could tell they were both angry. Slowly Fliberty smiled and gave a nod and a wink. Then he extended his hands to cast a shadow on the wall. Heddy winked back and quietly pushed Oinkey and me over to Fliberty's bellows. I knew what we had to do.

The swindlers were busy counting their money and laughing. Short Tooth looked up and said, "Hey, Captain, what's got into that dog?"

Samson's hair stood on end. He crouched down and bared his teeth.

"C-C-Captain?" Short Tooth stammered. "What's that behind you?"

The Captain turned and saw a monstrous shadow on the wall. It had jaws that opened and closed and huge fangs. "Whish! Whish! Whish!" it breathed. "BAM! BAM! BAM!" it stomped. "EEEE-Haw! EEEE-Haw!!" it roared. "EEEEEE! EEEEE!!" it screeched.

"That's a REAL monster! QUICK! LET'S GET OUT OF HERE!" Short Tooth screamed. They jumped up and ran off as fast as they could.

Fliberty, Aunt Heddy and I started laughing and could not stop for the longest time.

When Aunt Heddy took me home, Mama was amazed to hear what had happened. I will feel safe when I sleep tonight, knowing that there is no such thing as an Adapulgus creeping around outside.

Saturday

This morning I went over to Fliberty's.

"Lucky, go find everybody who went to see the Adapulgus last night," he said. "Tell them to show up at my place as soon as they can."

I did as he asked. There were lots of people at Ravenell's General Store. I let them know that Fliberty wanted to see them.

I told Jasper and the folks having breakfast at Payne's Inn. I told Old Hans and the McGintys. On the way back, I met Aunt Heddy and Oinkey and I told them, too.

Fliberty's place began to fill up with folks. They all wanted to know what was going on. So did I.

I knew Fliberty was too modest to boast about how he'd tricked the Captain. But what could be so important? We didn't have to wait long. Fliberty explained how there was no Adapulgus. He said the Captain had fooled us all into buying a ticket when there was nothing to see except a curtain shaking and some loud hollering by those two swindlers.

Some in the crowd nodded their heads. Some got mad and some just looked at the ground, ashamed of being bamboozled.

Then Fliberty held up a sack of coins. It was the same sack Captain Ragg had taken out of his vest.

"For all his big talk, that big man left town in such a hurry that he dropped his precious loot. Found it this morning," Fliberty said.

He gave everyone their money back. That seemed to make them feel a little better.

"What made those two run out of town so fast that they left the sack of money behind?" Old Hans asked.

"Well, maybe it was their own imagination that scared them off," Fliberty said.

I looked over at Aunt Heddy and Oinkey. It was all we could do to keep from laughing.

"It's too bad you weren't with us last night," I whispered to Jasper. "You would have enjoyed seeing Captain Ragg and that Short Tooth get a dose of their own medicine."

Then we saw the old dog, Samson, creep in. "Don't worry, friends, he's alone," Fliberty told us. "He's been hanging around all day. He can stay with me if he wants."

Samson wagged his tail. Then he jumped up and landed right on top of the bellows. It gave a puff of air and made the donkeys kick. "Eee-Haw!" "Whish! Bam!!" Then Oinkey squealed, "EEEEEE," and everybody laughed. That made us all feel a lot better.

This has been a true account of how the Adapulgus came and left Cobtown in the year 1845.

I hereby sign this,

✳ Lucky Hart ✳

EAGLE · DOG

BULL · DONKEY

ROOSTER · GOAT

RABBIT · SWAN

THE COBTOWN OBSERVER

I.B. HOOTIE: CHIEF CORRESPONDENT, EDITOR, PRINTER AND PUBLISHER.

MYSTERY MONSTER COMES TO COBTOWN!

This Friday evening, we will be treated to a look at an, until now, unknown beast. According to its owner, one Capt. Ragg, it is an ADAPULGUS (Add-a-*pull*-guss). This rare monster was captured in the Indian Territory. It took a large party of hunters to subdue the beast, as it has a fierce nature and great strength. Capt. Ragg claims that he and his associate, Short Tooth, have just recently begun to show the monster. That, he says, could be the reason why nobody hereabouts has ever heard of the creature. This lack of knowledge can be remedied on Friday evening at six o'clock, when the Captain and Mr. Tooth

will offer Cobtown the "once-in-a-lifetime opportunity" to view the living (and *very* heavily restrained) Adapulgus. It will be on display in a tent down in the Beaver Meadow. A fee of 25 cents will be charged to see the monster. The public is urged to stay clear of that area until exhibition time for their own safety. ✶ ✶ ✶ ✶ ✶ ✶

McGINTY ON THE MONSTER

We asked Professor Cornelius McGinty, of McGinty's Museum and Olio of Oddities here in Cobtown, for his thoughts on this monster. He replied: "Although I have never encountered an *Adapulgus* in all my explorations of Natural Philosophy, I do not discount its existence. Far stranger creatures have walked the earth and swum the seas than we can e'er imagine. For a modest token of only *five* (5) cents, the public may amaze and educate itself at McGinty's Museum. Therein they will gaze in wonder at our display of Vegetable Oddities; be awed by our rare collection of Mermaid Teeth; and be thrilled by the spectacle of 'The History of the Natural World,' in six paintings by Madam McGinty. To deprive oneself of such an experience would be a crime against Nature! Refreshments available."